A Forbidden Fruit Novella

TEMPTING GRAYSON

DANI RENÉ

BLURB

She's younger. She's off limits. She's forbidden.
But it doesn't stop me wanting her.

We flirt innocently. This is what we do.
Only... It's wrong.
That's what I tell myself.

I shouldn't be craving and needing.
She shouldn't be blushing and trembling.

We shouldn't be doing this... thing.

Why? Because she's... forbidden fruit.

PROLOGUE

You can't stop your heart from wanting someone.

You can't stop your mind from thinking about someone.

You can't stop your body craving someone.

Even if it's forbidden.

I should know, I've felt it for three years.

I shouldn't want him or dream about him, and I certainly shouldn't fantasize about his incredible body with those lips that utter my name as if he's consuming a savory treat. His gaze that pins me to the spot, rooted there just for him to greedily devour.

I first laid eyes on him when I was thirteen, too young to notice, and too innocent to know. However, when I hit sixteen and got my first boyfriend, that's when it slowly started to sink in that I wanted nobody else but him.

We spoke every day. He'd text me sweet messages. I'd giggle. He'd chuckle.

Our eyes would meet across the room, just like in the movies, in fairy tales, but this wasn't a happily ever after, and he wasn't meant to be my prince. Even so, I'd get that flurry of butterflies that seemed to be around every time he was. Over the years, when I went to family events with my parents, he'd be there. As if he could feel my eyes on him, he'd turn to regard me. With those dark brown eyes piercing me, boring into me, and that sinful smirk that had my cotton panties wet.

The first time I brought a boy home, he was there, beside my stepdad, and something in his glare told me I wasn't the only one with jealousy coursing through my veins.

Two days later, he came around with a blonde bimbo hanging off his arm, offering me a smirk that told me he did it on purpose. Seeing his hands on her, his lips on hers broke my heart. I locked myself in my bedroom till they left. It might have been childish, but I couldn't stand being in the same room as them, seeing him flirt with her.

Shaking my head of the memories of that dinner, I try to focus on the book in front of me.

I'm lying in bed and studying when my phone buzzes beside me.

It's him.

Grayson Connor.

Sliding my finger across the screen, I open the message and smile.

Grayson: You're a sweetheart. Don't let him break your heart. Or I will have to kill him.

Hitting reply, I lie back and tap out a message.

Me: Can't be having that. I'd miss you if you're locked up and I couldn't see you.

This is what we do.

We flirt. It's innocent enough.

Only . . .

It's not.

I shouldn't feel a flutter of excitement. I shouldn't be blushing or grinning.

We shouldn't be doing this . . . Thing.

Why?

Because Grayson Connor is my stepfather's brother.

MILA

"What do you think you're doing, young lady?" The deep, low growl stills all movement, and my heart ricochets wildly in my chest.

I inhale a deep breath before pivoting on my stupid four-inch heels. Only because my friends decided to dress up did I wear these god-awful shoes. I regard the dark-haired man leaning against the kitchen island in the dim light of the full moon.

It's almost two in the morning, and I've tried being as stealthy as possible, but obviously, someone's stalking me. It's been like this nearly every time he stays over. And since Daddy has gone into business with his brother, I'm stuck in a warp of wanting Grayson and not being able to have him.

So, instead, I tempt him every chance I get. But the man has the will of a fucking saint. Yes, he's a man-whore. That's no secret, but I wish he'd see me as a woman and not a little girl.

Rolling my eyes, I set my purse on the counter, sigh, and ignore him. I shouldn't have to explain myself. I'm nineteen, an adult. Yet he treats me like a fucking child.

I head to the fridge to grab a bottle of chilled water. As I shut the door, I feel his dark gaze boring into my back. The heat singing me, and there's no mistaking how much I'm affected by him.

"I asked you a question." He's behind me, so close, in fact, I can feel his heartbeat thrumming against my back. Hands grip my tiny hips, and he tugs me back against him. The rounded curve of my ass is now pressing against what I can feel is a thick, hard erection.

He's hard for me. The realization makes me grin, and thankfully, he can't see the grin on my face.

"You know I don't like it when you ignore me,

Mila." His low, angry tone shudders through me, and I have to close my eyes to keep my body from betraying me. *Shit.* She's a bitch because I'm already trembling and needy. The ache between my thighs is already tightening, swirling with desire for the man I can't have. My pussy pulses, begging for something I have imagined but only he can deliver.

"Why do you care? You're not my father, Grayson." I hiss my response, causing him to push me away quickly as if I've scorched him. "What are you doing here anyway?" My anger isn't warranted, but my jealousy is. I saw him earlier in the same nightclub my friends and I walked into. He was sitting between two pretty women who were practically naked.

"I do care," he promises, his tone turning urgent, honesty blazing in his eyes. Even in the dim light, I can see Grayson cares for me. "I'm here because your father and I have a meeting early tomorrow." He lifts a hand and rakes it through his dark brown hair, causing another wave of desire to flush through me at an alarming rate. My heart leaps into my throat when he pins me with those mocha eyes.

"I'm nineteen, legal, and an adult. You have no right to question me." The words fall from my lips before I have time to think. His eyes heat, and even in the dark, I'm hooked, caught in a web of self-destruction, because the only thing I can think of is leaping into his arms and wrapping my legs around his taut waist.

"You may be legal, Mila, but I'll be damned if I stand by watching you go out partying and fucking every boy in the neighborhood. Your father would have a fucking stroke if he knew." The word *fuck* in his smooth, silky, whispered baritone is enough to have my panties drenched with arousal.

The thought of Grayson knowing I'm no longer the sweet, innocent girl he's watched grow up makes me wish I could've hidden it away. I'm not sure why, but the confusing desire courses through me, wanting him to see me as a woman, but also wanting him to remember me as the girl who needed him through the darkest time in her life.

I know my feelings aren't normal. They can't be, but I can't stop them. Each time I see him, when he saunters into the house, I'm a teenager with a crush.

When my stepdad married my mother, I'd just turned thirteen, and when I first met his brother, I gawked. It's wrong, so fucking wrong, but god, I can't help but ache whenever I'm near him. Now, at nineteen, he's the only man I picture when I slide my hand between my legs.

My uncle elicits feelings from me that I can't explain. The burst of wings that tickle my belly when Grayson walks into the room and the ache in my core has me quivering when I think of his hands on me.

I can't even tell any of my friends about it because I'm afraid of the judgment, and I can't even imagine what Aunt Shanika will say.

"Fine, I won't go around fucking *every* boy I see, if you give me some privacy." I stalk past him, thinking it's done, when suddenly he grips my arm, tugging me against his rock-hard body. For a thirty-two-year-old man, he's built better than any of my college friends. And the ink that adorns his arms only adds to his allure.

"Do not use that tone with me, sweetheart," he bites out close to my ear, sending electric sparks trailing through every inch of my body.

"Why? Are you going to put me over your knee and spank me, Uncle Grayson?" I quip playfully, but the way his eyes glower tells me he's considering it. Squeezing my thighs together, I bite my lip to keep from moaning as the images play out in my mind. *Fuck, I'd love for him to do that.*

"Don't tempt me, sweetheart. I'm not averse to

doing just that."

Suddenly, he releases me and stalks down the hallway toward the guest bedroom. When the door clicks in the darkness, I release the breath I'd been holding. But the scent of his masculine cologne hangs heavily in the air.

I toe off my heels and pad down the opposite hallway and up the stairs which lead to my bedroom, still reeling from the interaction with him. I'm in so much trouble as each time I'm near him, my feelings only seem to taunt me further. Pushing the door to my bedroom open, I step inside and shut it behind me.

Thoughts of what Grayson Connor does to me is wrong on so many levels, but I push him to do it. I tease him mercilessly. Shoving off my pink miniskirt, I glance in the mirror. I've always been curvy, with my hips wider than my waist. My breasts are bigger than any of my friends', and I always wondered if Grayson didn't prefer those petite girls because they were the opposite of me.

My long, black hair hangs in waves down my back. My olive skin gives me a year-round tan, and boys hit on me all the time. Too bad the only man I want is forbidden.

When my mother passed away three years ago, I admit, I went off the deep end. The only man who understands me is my uncle. He was the one who was there to listen to me cry, to hear me confess how much it hurt that she's no longer around. I've had him to confide in for so long, and he's been amazing, giving me advice and helping me through the worst.

My stepfather, on the other hand, is the complete opposite, because he would lock me away in a tower if he could. As long as I have my phone, I'll still be able to talk to Grayson. I know my uncle's younger than most, and perhaps that's why he gets me, but I know I wouldn't have been able to get through the three years after losing my mother if it weren't for him.

Somehow, over the time we'd grown closer, I'd lost my heart to him. I've fallen, and there's no way back up. I'm head over fucking heels. So, whenever he tells me about yet another notch on his bedpost, I go off the deep end, finding some willing college boy who'll allow me to be his arm candy, and I do it only to make Grayson jealous.

I know dreams of him will haunt me tonight, and I'll wake up with my hand between my thighs until I find relief. Only, the desire never abates. It just grows stronger. Images of being under one of the most important men in my life have me once again pulsing with need.

Is it wrong to want your uncle to fuck you?

Because I want Grayson Connor to do just that.

But is it wrong to want to make love to him too?

Yes, it is.

All I have to live with are the what ifs.

GRAYSON

Last night, when I caught Mila sneaking in after curfew, I wanted to tell her father, but I know my brother, and he'll only worry. So, I decided I won't say anything to Gabe just yet. I'm concerned she's still acting like a rogue teenager.

After three years of being her shoulder to cry on, her advisor, and the person who's always been there for her in the roughest of times, I feel as if I have a responsibility to keep her secrets, but I'm grown up enough to know if she does do something stupid, I'll be there to catch her.

It's just hit six in the morning, the sun is just peeking through the windows, and I've been in my brother's gym for almost an hour. Working out has always helped clear my mind when it comes to Mila, but I can't stop the thoughts of her in that tiny mini skirt she wore last night. She had me rock fucking hard, and I rushed to my room to jerk off, thinking about how her ass felt pressed against my dick.

Lifting the weight, I can't help watching the sweat drip from my chest. Before I have time to think any more about last night, the door swings open, and Mila's hourglass figure strolls over the threshold. She's dressed in Lycra leggings and a sports bra. Her long hair is tied into a messy bun, and she looks like sin.

"Morning, Grayson," she coos, and I know she's trying to taunt me. She loves it, yet she doesn't realize I know exactly what she's doing.

"Mila," I grunt, and with great difficulty, I drag my gaze from her and concentrate on what I'm doing. The mirror allows me to drink in her perfect form as she straddles the spinning machine while my cock thickens imagining her riding me.

Get a fucking grip.

"What are you doing today?" she questions without meeting my eyes in the mirror. Her voice soft and melodic, and I bend over, having to put the weights down before I kill myself by dropping them.

"Your father and I are meeting a supplier, but I'm heading in early because I need to get the paperwork to the office first. Then I'm having lunch with Colette," I add on, knowing she hates the woman I've been seeing on and off for the past two months. But it's merely an agreement of no-strings fun. Yet, each time Colette joins me here at the house, Mila's face glowers with anger.

I realized early on it was jealousy, and I played it to my advantage.

It may be juvenile, but when Mila brings her boy-toys home, I'm rabid. We play this game of cat and mouse, and each day my restraint slips a little more. The need to pull her across my lap and spank her pert little ass is enough to have me straining in my boxers every time she's around.

To mark that smooth, olive skin with my handprint is tempting, too fucking tempting. Turning, I head toward the door. Stopping at the bike as I watch her for a moment.

"She's so wrong for you, Grayson." Her pout is

adorable, and I regard her with a smirk.

"And why is that, sweetheart?" Crossing my arms in front of my chest, I watch her gaze trail down my torso.

"Because, she's just not right for you. I don't have to have a reason."

Leaning in close to her, I hear the hitch in her breathing. Her chest heaves as her movements falter. "And who would you suggest I fuck?" I study her carefully and notice her squirm at the word *fuck*. I'd love to bend her over this machine and drive into her.

"Someone other than her," she grits out in frustration, turning up the bike a notch to an uphill climb, and I wonder if she's working out her frustration the same way I've done. But then again, the thought of her lying in her bed rubbing her pussy, thinking of me, doesn't help my erection. She turns her head in indignation and meets my gaze.

"Well, if that's how you feel, tell me exactly why you don't like her, and I may reconsider." I lean in farther, planting a soft kiss on her cheek, and I whisper in her ear, "I'll even reward you for your effort." With that, I leave her in the gym and think about what I just offered.

In the guest bedroom, I head into the *en suite* and push down my shorts and boxer briefs. My cock is hard, and it's all the little kitten's fault. She does things to me that I should deny. I should tell her it's wrong, but I can't find the words when she's near me.

Even our messages have become something of an addiction for me. At first, it started innocently. And over the years, she's become more than just a teenager I remember meeting when Gabe married her mom.

She's a woman.

All fucking woman.

Pushing the button on the automated shower system, I wait a moment for it to heat before stepping under the warm spray.

Every muscle in my body is tense, needing relief and release. Gripping my shaft, I stroke it to images of her in those tiny skirts she loves to flaunt her ass in. Her breasts — a perfect handful — taunt me from her skin-tight tank tops. Her long, jet-black hair, which I'd love to wrap around my fist while I'm pounding into her for being a naughty little girl, has my body shuddering with a release that elicits a groan from my mouth.

Opening my eyes, I lather up and try to wash the

memories of what I've just done away; however, I know I can't. Once I've rinsed the suds away, I turn off the shower and step out into the chilly bathroom, grabbing a towel. Wrapping it around my waist, I place both hands on the basin and stare at my appearance.

When did it all change?

How did she weave herself inside me?

I'm a man-whore, I love women, I love pussy, but right now, the only one I want is her. It's been a life of being the playboy, but the thought of doing that doesn't please me anymore. What does bring me satisfaction, is seeing Mila smile.

"Grayson." A sweet, melodic voice jolts me into the present, and I turn in time to find Mila standing in the doorway. "Can I get a ride to the mall? If you're going into town?"

She's changed already, dressed in a white tank top that hugs her tits like a glove, and a pair of shorts which stop high on her slender thighs. A pair of ballet flats adorn her pretty feet, and her long hair is loose down her back in waves.

"Sure, sweetheart." Stepping toward the door, her green eyes flit down my chest, which is still wet from the shower. Heat burns in those moss-colored pools.

"Was there something else?" I question, my body only inches from hers.

She peers up at me with wide, innocent eyes. Her small frame would fit perfectly in mine. "I, uhm . . ." Her words taper off, and I wait for it, hoping with everything I am she'll say something, to give me consent to kiss her. "I'm sorry about last night. And thank you for giving me a lift."

They're not the words I want. The hope that was bubbling in my chest dies like a dried-out bud, and I know I can't do much unless she gives me the response I need.

"You don't have to apologize, sweetheart. I just worry about you. And you know I'd do anything for you." I lean in, inhaling her scent. Sweet like candy, bubblegum, and cookies. And I'll be damned, but I want to taste her.

"Anything?" she questions in a sultry, honeyed tone. The playful flirting immerges quickly, and her eyes sparkle with mischief. The air is thick with swirling desire, so thick you could cut it with a knife.

Closing the distance between us, I murmur, "That's what I said, Mila. I'm yours." My tone is low and gruff against her ear. "So, you're welcome to take what you need."

The promise is so evident, so fucking clear what I want and need from her. Chill bumps dot her smooth skin, and I can't help the smirk that lifts the side of my mouth.

"I'll remember that, Uncle Grayson," she murmurs so quietly I would have missed it if we weren't so close. I step away, and just like that, the spell is broken.

"Good girl." I step past her, strolling into my walk-in closet, and retrieve a pair of boxers. When Gabe told me we'd be working together more often, he offered me space in one of the guest rooms. Being so close to Mila was a perk, and I didn't refuse when he told me I could move some of my things in.

Awareness prickles my skin the moment I straighten to full height. I know she's still close. Dropping the towel, I step into my underwear, and a faint, audible gasp comes from behind me, and I realize she was closer than I thought.

I turn slowly, hoping to catch her in the act, but when my gaze lands on the door, it's empty. She must have scurried off after getting an eyeful, and I can't stop the satisfied chuckle that rumbles through my chest.

MILA

Jesus, his ass.

Fuck.

Oh. My. God.

As soon as I'm in the safety of my bedroom, I lean against the door and try to calm my heart rate. I don't know if he knew I was there, but my feet were cemented, and as much as I wanted to run, I couldn't. His body looked like it was carved out of marble. Thick, muscled thighs, an ass you could probably bounce a quarter off, and his back chiseled

21

to panty-melting perfection.

He's your uncle, Mila.

Well, step-uncle, if that's even a thing.

As much as that mantra replays itself in my head, I can't stop the dirty thoughts of him from running through my mind. A knock at my door jolts me from the images.

"Sweetheart, you ready?" His deep, gruff voice calls to me.

"Yes, I'll be out in a minute," I respond, hoping to have a moment to myself.

"Okay, I'll be in the kitchen. Don't be too long. I need to get going."

"Yes, Grayson . . ." I drag out his name, which earns me a chuckle, and I'm sure he's shaking his head at me.

Even though I have a physical reaction to him, it's also my heart that seems to be aching each time I see him with someone else. I can't love him. I mean, of course, he's family, and I love that he's around, but . . . Can I really fall in love with a man I can't have?

Grabbing my phone and purse, I make my way down to the kitchen to find him drinking his coffee. "I'm ready when you are. Where's Dad?"

Lifting his gaze, he corners me with those deep,

chocolate pools. God, how I would love to drown in them. "He's getting ready now. He'll meet me at the office," he responds quickly before downing the last of his drink and grabbing his keys and wallet. As we head out to the car, I can't help dragging my gaze over the way his shirt hugs his chiseled torso.

When he's working with Dad, he's styled with formal dress shirts and suits, along with a tie that always matches his handkerchief in the breast pocket of his jacket. However, when he's on a night out, it's an experience in itself to see him in jeans and T-shirts that always seem to be painted on his muscular body.

He pulls out of the driveway in silence. Something in the air has the hairs on the nape of my neck raised in anticipation. Reaching over, I turn on the radio, hoping the music will drown out the silence.

"I want to get a tattoo." The confession spills from my lips, and I turn my inquisitive gaze to his. He doesn't flinch, eyes trained on the road ahead.

"And what is it you'd like inked on your skin forever, sweetheart?" he questions with an indifferent tone.

I shrug. "I want something small. Nothing over the top, since Dad would kill me." I smirk playfully at the thought of having the tattoo on me forever.

"And when you're tired of having it, then you'll want it removed," he responds confidently, but still doesn't meet my gaze. "Where did you plan on getting this tattoo?"

"It's a surprise. I think I'll get it today." Lifting my chin, I inform him of my decision, waiting on a reaction which doesn't come. All he does is nod.

When we pull up to the mall, he turns a darkened gaze on me. His mouth lifts on one side into a wolfish grin that turns my insides molten. "You do realize your father is going to have a fit when he sees his little girl with ink on her?"

"Possibly, but where I'm planning on getting it, Daddy won't see it," I quip playfully with a wink. Hopping out of the car, I blow him a kiss and make my way into the large building that houses an array of stores with incredible designer clothes and a couple of bookstores. There's even a large cinema. Although, that's not why I'm here. My appointment is in ten minutes, so I make my way directly to Rusted Ink.

Stepping into the intimidating store, I take in the deep blue and red colors that decorate the walls and chairs. There's only one other person sitting on the sofa in the waiting area as I approach the counter.

"Can I help you?" A thick, husky voice beckons for me, and when I turn around, I'm knocked breathless.

The man must be in his late twenties with dark stubble dusting his jaw. A deep set of green eyes, the color of grass, pin me to the spot, holding me hostage as if he's got his hands all over me. Tattoos cover every inch of visible skin, and I find myself licking my lips involuntarily.

"You can. I, uhm . . . I've made an appointment for ten o'clock to get a tattoo." I step forward, holding out the email confirmation. He glances at the book in front of him and nods.

"Mila," he affirms in a smoky tone. "I'll be doing you today. What are you getting, and where do you want it?" His question catches me off guard because of the way he says it doesn't sound like he's talking about a tattoo, more like an invitation to find out what he's hiding in his boxers.

I may look innocent, but I'm far from it, so I know when a man's tone changes from an everyday one to a low, growly rasp that's filled with lust. That's how I know Grayson wants me because I've heard it in his voice before.

"I'm getting the word *sweetheart* on my lower abdomen, just beneath my belly button. I want a script font that looks like handwriting." I point to where my shorts currently hang low on my waist, and he nods.

"Great. Let's get you in the back." He pushes off the stool, and as soon as I enter through the black door, the sound of a needle buzzing grabs my attention. There are two cubicles separated by curtains, and the tattooed man ushers me into the empty one on the left. He points to the empty bed. "Lie down and shift those shorts down so I can see what I'm working with." He heads back into the main area of the store while I close my eyes, inhaling deep breaths.

Hooking my thumbs in the waistband of my shorts, I shrug them down just enough for him to be able to see where I want to be inked. When he returns with his phone in hand, his green eyes take in my position, and his gaze darkens considerably when he notices the sheer black material of my panties.

He doesn't say a word while he works, cleaning the area on either side of my hip bones and along my stomach, which is fluttering with nervous energy. "Did you have a personal preference on color, or are you happy with just black?" I notice he's got two printouts of the script I sent them when I made my booking.

"Black is perfect. Thank you." I offer a shy smile, and I'm afforded a wicked one in return. One that slowly disintegrates my nerves and has my heart thudding in my chest.

My father is going to kill me, but I can't deny the thrill of doing something forbidden. I close my eyes and think of Grayson's hungry gaze filled with desire. Soon, he'll see me as a woman, and then I'll make sure he shows me exactly how badly he wants to spank me.

GABRIEL

"Is that all you needed from me?" My brother nods. The meeting went well since we've just signed a deal with an affluent software company to have them on our books. We'll be doing all their marketing and upcoming branding campaign.

"Yeah, they'll email us the finalized contract, and we're good to go," he affirms with a nod. Grayson and I didn't have the easiest childhood growing up, and since we partnered up to open Connor Media, we've grown closer. "I wanted to take my niece out for her birthday," he says smoothly, meeting my gaze. I know he loves younger women, and my protective instincts kick in when he mentions Mila.

"Oh?" My response clipped, and I get the look. He narrows his dark eyes, fixing them on me. Even though he's younger, he's got a good head on his shoulders. At thirty-two, he's four years my junior, but the way he conducts business, you'd never guess.

"I figured since you'll be taking Brigitte to Miami that weekend, I could take Mila somewhere special." We've had this conversation too many times. He knows how I feel about her being alone with him. His feelings for her have shifted over the past few years, and since she's turned nineteen, I've seen the way she looks at him.

"Is that a good idea? Being alone with her?" Grabbing my phone and wallet, I push off the chair and stalk around the desk but don't meet his stare. My phone rings and I ignore him and swipe my finger over the screen. "Hello, Princess," I murmur, even though I know he can hear me.

"Dad, I'm done. So, whenever you're ready, I'll wait at entrance four." Her tone is chirpy like she's up to no good, which I can only imagine is the tattoo Grayson mentioned earlier. "Oh, and say hello to

Uncle Grayson." She giggles before hanging up.

"Look, I know what you're thinking, but I'm responsible. She will be safe with me, and we have fun." He chuckles, but I pin him with an angry glare.

"Don't be an asshole. You think I don't notice the flirting between you two?" He doesn't respond, only laughs, but the twinkle in his eyes tells me all I need to know. "I need to go."

"Tell her Uncle Grayson says he's bringing her some treats this weekend," the gruff tone of my brother calls after me as I head out the door. I don't respond; he's acting like a pompous ass, as usual.

Slipping into the plush leather seat of my Benz, I turn on Mila's favorite playlist on the iPod and head toward the mall. I know she's gotten a tattoo, and if I have to be honest, I can't fault her for it. She's an adult, and even if I denied her getting one, she'd do it anyway.

Since her mother died three years ago, I've wanted her to move in with her aunt, her mother's sister, but she refused. Saying she'd rather spend time in the home where her mother was last. It made her feel closer to the woman she lost. I wanted her away from Grayson, but if she's adamant he's the one for her, I'll support them, just as long as my brother turns his life around.

Even though there were times she frustrated me with her rebelliousness, she's never been a disruptive teen. As a child, she preferred sitting in her bedroom reading or working on her art projects. She now has two months before she heads off to college, and I'm afraid. I'll never admit it, but I'd prefer if she stayed in the city, went to study at a local school rather than head off to New York or someplace where I can't see her every day.

Pulling up to the mall, I find entrance four easily. Before the car comes to a stop, Mila comes bounding toward the car with the biggest grin on her face. She pulls the door open, and I see her wince. "Hello, Dad." She leans in, and her candy floss scent hits me immediately. Planting a chaste kiss on my cheek, she sits back to regard me. "How's Uncle Grayson?"

"Fine." I can't help feeling a twinge of wariness at their connection. I'm not scared of her loving him. I just want him to make a choice. If it is Mila he wants, it should only be her he's with. They're not related by blood, and I don't know how to handle seeing them together. Because deep down, I know Grayson cares for her. More than I'd like to admit.

"Just fine? How was the meeting?" She's always

been interested in our work, and I have a feeling she'll major in advertising, which makes me proud I've had such a profound effect on her.

"It went well. We signed the deal. We'll be doing all their marketing and rebranding," I tell her proudly as we head home. The song changes and she squeals in delight at the band on the radio.

"That's great. I wish I could work for you," she murmurs, and I cut a quick glance at her. She pouts playfully, and I can't help chuckling. I'd like that too, and I'm sure my brother wouldn't mind at all.

"You can if you'd like to, of course?" I hint, and her gaze darts to mine.

She blushes shyly, her voice lower when she responds, "I do, but I'll need to finish school first."

I nod in agreement. Broaching the subject, I answer cautiously, "Then why not stay in Seattle to study?" We've spoken about this when she was sixteen, and even when she'd turned seventeen, but she's always refused.

She's quiet for a long while, and I feel as if I fucked it up.

I pull into our driveway and park the car. Once the engine is turned off, I turn to face her fully. "Mila, I didn't mean to—"

"Yes." Her deep green pools regard me. A smile lights up her face. "I'd like to stay here, in Seattle I mean, and with you." Her voice drops on those last two words, and I tip my head to the side.

"You do?"

"Why wouldn't I?" She turns and once again, I see the wince.

"Are you okay, Princess? You look like you're in pain?" I question calmly, knowing exactly why. I wonder if she'll tell me about the goddamn tattoo Grayson told me about.

"I'll show you inside. Let's go, I'm hungry," Mila says quietly. Without waiting for me, she pushes her door open and leaves me in the car staring after her. Exiting the Benz, I lock it and follow my princess up to the house. When I enter, she's in the kitchen leaning against the island drinking a glass of juice.

"So," I prompt, stalking toward her, keeping my eyes trained on her. "Am I going to see how you mutilated your body?" Her eyes widen in shock, and her mouth drops open, and then closes again. "I'm not stupid, Mila, and I wasn't born yesterday. Let's see." I gesture with my chin.

I have tattoos, and a piercing which was a drunken mistake; however, after I got it done, my girlfriend didn't complain, so I kept it. Even Mila's mother enjoyed the sensation.

Watching my little girl unbutton her shorts has me wondering just what the hell she did. My heart hammers against my rib cage painfully, and I have to stifle a groan when she shoves her shorts down just below her panty line. There, between her hip bones, is the word sweetheart.

Jesus. Fucking. Christ.

"You got a fucking tattoo, Mila?" I growl. Her head snaps up so fast, and her brows furrow in confusion at my outburst. *Fuck.* Even I'm confused at my outburst. But I realize it's not that she got it, it's that she must have had to drop her pants for a stranger. I hope to god it was a woman who did the ink on her body.

"I thought you—"

"Tell me it was a woman who did it?" Scrubbing my hands over my scruffy jaw, I try to calm myself down, but the image of my daughter lying on a table while some fucker touched her drives me fucking crazy.

"God, what the fuck is wrong with you?" she suddenly bursts out. Through the haze of anger, I glance up and find her glaring at me.

"What did you just say to me?" My voice is

controlled, low and gravelly, and from the expression on my face, she must know I'm livid.

"Nothing . . .," she pouts, but this time I'm not falling for her little girl act. If she wants to be an adult, she better start acting like one. So many times over the past year, I've looked at her and seen not my little girl, but a woman. An adult. Someone who challenges me. When I was married to Louisa, I didn't look at another woman, let alone entertain the thought of growing old with anyone but her. When she died, my world collapsed around me. It was Mila who dragged me from the dark to the light. Her light.

"Mila Reyes do not ignore me," I command, and her eyes meet mine.

"I'm not. I'm just tired of you looking at me like a fucking child." The curse word falling from her lips doesn't anger me like a parent should. It makes me want to chuckle at how much my daughter has grown up.

"If you use that word in front of me one more time, you will get a spanking, and you'll not be able to sit down for a week. Or did you want your Uncle Grayson to do it?" I'm almost in her face as I bite out my question, and her mouth gapes in shock. She doesn't know that I know about her conversations and flirting with him, but when I meet her indignant stare, I know it's obvious.

She pushes past me, but before she's out of earshot, I hear it. "Just stay out of my life, Daddy."

MILA

"Just stay out of my life, Daddy." My murmur must have reached him because suddenly I'm being yanked backward.

"Mila, just know if you want to cross that line with him, there is no going back," he growls, his lips inches from my ear. I don't respond because I don't trust my words. Instead, I push back and run into my bedroom, ignoring the shock that slowly envelopes me.

My father knows. Was I that obvious about it? Did

Grayson say anything to him? The doorbell dings through the house, and I curl around my pillow. I wish Dad didn't invite that woman over he's been seeing. Brigitte. I can't stand her. She's as fake as a damn Barbie doll, and I'm over seeing him waste his time with her.

Before I have time to think, my bedroom door flies open, and Grayson Connor is standing there looking as delicious as he did this morning. His shirt is unbuttoned, and the cuffs are rolled up to his elbows. "Gabe says you're in here pouting about the tattoo," he quips with a smirk. Mischief sparkles in his gaze, and I can't help shaking my head.

"I'm in here because he's being obtuse, and he also knows about us." He doesn't deny it; instead, he nods and takes a step inside, shutting the door behind him.

"Come here, Mila," he orders in a tone so rough I feel the words ripple over my skin. Rolling over, I push off the bed and take a tentative step toward him. "Closer," he growls. Yes, he growled. Once our bodies are flush, he reaches for my wrists and pulls me against him. "Let me see your ink."

Releasing me, he steps back, and I gently shove the shorts down an inch to show him the script that adorns my stomach just below my belly button. Another rumble comes from him, and when I meet those molten chocolate eyes, they burn into me.

Swiftly, he grabs me and spins me around, pressing me against the wall beside my bedroom door. The soft lavender is so close to my face; it looks white. "Are you mine, sweetheart?" he whispers over my cheek. I don't respond. Instead, I press my ass against his crotch. The thick hardness of his cock is evident, and I can't help biting my lip and moaning like a wanton little slut.

Generally, his thick Scottish accent drives me crazy, but now that he's murmuring in my ear, I can't stop the illicit thoughts from running rampant through my mind.

A low growl rumbles in his chest. "Do you think rubbing your little ass on my cock is going to get you out of a spanking?"

"Maybe," I murmur, my voice breathy as I respond with a shiver skittering down my spine.

"You're sorely mistaken, Mila, because Uncle Grayson is going to teach you just what naughty girls get when they're bad."

Jesus.

My thighs squeeze together in eager anticipation.

Desire coils low in my stomach, tightening everything below my belly button. Before I can answer, he spins me in his arms and presses my front to his. His cock pushes against my stomach, and I can't stop the moan that falls from my lips.

He leans in and murmurs in my ear, "My innocent, little sweetheart. I'm about to color those ass cheeks red, and then I'm going to make you purr."

With one small step back, he regards me with that filthy smirk curling his lips. He reaches for my hand and tugs me along as we head toward the bed.

He settles onto the mattress and tugs me over his lap. *Fuck. He's really doing it.*

A feather-light stroke down my spine, so slow it seems to seep through the cotton of my top heats my skin. He reaches my shorts, and with one big, rough hand, he grips my left cheek, squeezing it. "You have such a lovely little ass. I've wanted to spank you for a long time now, sweetheart," he confirms, his voice thick with desire. "Stand. I want to see those pretty panties you wore for me."

I manage to rise from his lap. Snapping my gaze to his, I gasp, "For you? You really think I wore these for you?" I ask incredulously.

"Of course you did." He grins confidently.

"I don't do everything for you."

"So, you don't lie in bed at night rubbing your little cunt for me?" The way he says *cunt* is probably the sexiest thing I've ever heard. His accent is making it even harder to resist. I don't answer. Instead, I obey his request.

Unbuttoning my shorts, I shove them down my legs, allowing them to pool at my feet. I step out of my ballet flats, and I tug my tank top up and over my head. I'm standing before him in only a pair of sheer, black panties and a bra to match.

"Is that what you wanted to see?" I ask insolently. My curvy frame along with my C-cup breasts seem to have him speechless. My nipples harden against the luxurious fabric under his intense scrutiny. Nothing could have prepared me for this. He reaches out, and with his index finger, strokes the ink on my skin.

"These are perfect." His reverent tone is more than I can handle, and I feel tears spring to my eyes. Without warning, he grips my hips, careful not to touch the sensitive scars, and tugs me onto his lap so I'm straddling him. "Look at me," he commands me in *that* tone once more, and when I meet those deep cocoa pools, they're filled with desire, darkening to an almost black.

"I am," I quip playfully. My hands grip his shoulders, and I can feel his muscles tense under my tender touch. My body trembles when he trails both hands up to my arms and my hips roll involuntarily against him with my heated core against his hard bulge.

"Jesus, Mila, we shouldn't. You shouldn't want me. Do you know that?" he asks, and I nod.

"I do." My confession earns me a pained expression. "But I love you." His gaze snaps to mine, and as I roll my hips, I realize his restraint is slowly slipping. The ebb and flow of our bodies remind me of waves in the ocean, back and forth as I continue to grind.

My head falls back, and my eyes flutter closed as I revel in the erotic yet taboo act. "Please," I mewl as his lips find my hardened buds through the soft material of my bra.

They're peaked painfully, and his groan does nothing to ease the tightness in my belly. As if a storm is rolling in and I'm about to be caught in the aftermath. Dad's right; there's no going back. A stinging swat lands on my ass, and I cry out.

"But knowing it's wrong, that's what makes you wet, doesn't it, sweetheart?" he questions, and I'm so far gone, so lost in the lust for him. A man. Not my uncle, but a man.

"Yes, Uncle Grayson." The words fall unbidden, and I ride the wave, slow and meticulous until I'm at the crest, needy and aching for release. For the orgasm I know is only an inch away, within my grasp.

"Come for me, sweetheart. Come on your uncle's cock," he growls, and even though he's not inside me yet, his words spur me on, pushing me to the edge, and I shatter. Completely.

"Oh, God!" I cry out. My body convulses as my release hits me deep in my core, rattling through me like a wave crashing on the shore.

The storm raging in my body slowly subsides, and when I open my eyes, I find him staring up at me in awe. As if he wants to worship me. And I'd let him.

We sit silently, in astonishment at what just happened. Brown eyes meeting green, wonderment and emotion are tightening in my chest. "I . . ." My words falter. I want to apologize, but I don't know what I'd be saying sorry for.

"That was the single most incredible moment of my life, Mila." Grayson's voice, tone, and words send heat tingling through me. My blood feels as if it's boiling with lust, but deep down I know it's more. It's love. I've loved him as a father figure for so long, and now when I look at him, the affection I feel, the love, is for a man I want as a lover.

"You . . . I mean . . . Shit." I drop my gaze to his mouth, and I watch the small grin playing on it, teasing me like he always does.

"Don't curse," he admonishes, but the grin on his lips tells me he loves me cursing.

"Why? Because you're going to fuck me?" Lifting my finger, I slowly trail it over the stubble on his chin in a lazy, teasing move. Swiftly, he grips my wrist and brings my finger to his lips.

Pressing a soft kiss on the tip, he releases my wrist and reaches for my face. His big hand cups my cheek and swipes a thumb over my lips. "I'm going to kiss you now. This isn't going to be the same as the kisses we've shared before, Mila. There are so many reasons I shouldn't, and that I should let you go find a boy your own age, or even one that you haven't known since you were a teenager and forget this ever happened, but I can't. I crave you like a fucking drug, and I'm tired of denying myself a fix. I need you to know, sweetheart, this isn't only a one-night thing. If we do this, I want you. Only you," he confirms, but before I can ask what he means, his thumb pops between my lips, and I can't help sucking it into my mouth.

Flicking my tongue over it, I taunt him, and his eyes darken further. Desire pools in them, making them the color of dark chocolate and just as tempting.

"It's been a long two years watching you grow into a woman, and recently having these explicit feelings drives me to jerk my cock every day over fantasies of you in my mind." His filthy confession has arousal pooling between my legs, adding to the wetness already there from my orgasm.

"You're not the only one, Grayson," I murmur quietly.

"Good girl." With that, he cups both my cheeks and pulls my face toward him in a soul-searing kiss. His lips mold to mine, and his tongue delves into my mouth, fighting for dominance. He tastes of sin and taboo, yet he also tastes like pleasure and ecstasy. "You smell delectable, little one," he murmurs in my ear, and the shudder that slowly travels through my body is obvious. He wants me. I want him. Can this work?

I know this isn't going to be easy, but I want it more than anything.

"Uncle Grayson, your breathing on my neck is ticklish." I giggle playfully as his lips continue their descent to the curves of my breasts. He suckles, bites, and kisses me before gazing up again.

"As long as I hear that precious laugh from you, I'll do anything, sweetheart." His soft-spoken words cause me to smile so wide.

"Anything, Uncle Grayson?" I question, and his grin is pure sin. The way we're sitting, it's as if our bodies are made to fit together. He reaches for my face, his hand gripping my long black hair at the nape, and he tugs me toward his mouth.

Our lips only inches apart, he murmurs the words I've been dying to hear for far too long. "I'm going to feast on you, sweetheart, every supple inch of your body." A deep rumble comes from his chest, his mocha-colored eyes are almost black, and his lips form a smirk so devilish I can see how women fall to their knees for him.

Without warning, he grips my hips and rises easily. Turning around, he sets me on the bed, my back on the soft mattress with my legs on either side of his hips. He reaches for the waistband of my black, sheer panties and tugs them toward him. As he guides the soft material down my long, lithe legs, his gaze lingers on every inch of me. I watch as he rises, looking delectable as his shirt finds the floor in a soft whoosh. Large hands grip my hips, and he settles between my thighs.

We're both on the bed where I've spent many nights dreaming of him. My legs splay, and he stares in wonder at my slick core. I know Daddy is in the house, but right now, all I want is Grayson.

"Jesus," he grunts, his tone rough with desire, and my lips lift into a smirk.

"You shouldn't curse, Grayson," I tease playfully. "My uncle fucking hates me saying anything remotely curse-like." I lift my hand, biting down on my thumb.

"Sweetheart, you're going to be doing a lot more than cursing in a moment. I hope you're not shy about Gabe hearing you come because I'm going to make you scream my fucking name," he grunts, trying to keep his composure. The tiny bit of restraint falls away when his gaze falls on my pussy, which has a small patch of hair from my mound to my clit.

Grayson slides both his hands up and down my thighs as if he's massaging me, calming the electricity shooting through my veins, but it doesn't help, because I'm more turned on than I've ever been before.

A moan, so sexual, and so fucking erotic falls from my lips. "Please, Grayson," I beg, blatant and hungry.

He leans in, capturing my mouth in a soul-stealing kiss. There's nothing familial about it. This is a kiss of lovers, a man, and a woman. My body trembles, and when he breaks the contact, our eyes meet in a heated stare-down.

"Off with that bra, sweetheart. I want to see all of you," Grayson growls, his tone thick and demanding. "I'm starving, and I'm about to feast on that little cunt of yours. Do you want me to?" he taunts me, and I know he's loving every fucking second of it.

Quickly, without a second thought, I nod. No questions, no denying what we want, what we need. This is it. I'm stepping over the line, and I'm about to allow him to devour me.

I'm no longer his niece. I'm a woman he's about to taste.

GRAYSON

She's perfect. There isn't an inch of her I'm not going to touch, lick, bite, and fuck. She watches me intently with a small, shy smile on her plump lips. As soon as the flimsy material falls to the floor, her gaze rakes over me. I may not be chiseled like her little school friends, but I keep in shape with a daily gym routine and some night-time cardio that keeps me satisfied.

God, I've waited with baited-breath for so long, wanting every inch of her, wondering if I'd ever get

"Oh . . . Oh . . . God . . ." Her moans are mumbled as they tumble from her lips. Her fingers tug at my hair, pulling so hard the bite stings, but I don't care. I'm lost to the sensation of her body pulsing around my tongue. Her body locks, and a mewl, both decadent and erotic echoes around us, and I glance up to see her beautiful face as she unravels.

"So fucking sweet, my sweetheart," I murmur against her core. The sight of her glistening is enough to undo me right here in my fucking slacks.

Her gaze falls on me. Something in it tells me she feels it, our connection, and suddenly I'm jolted back to my past. A place I'd rather not go. I shake my head to clear the memories.

I focus on the here and now because I'm not sure if after this is all over, she'll still want me. That thought stings. It hurts, and I know why. I've let myself feel, fall . . . Fuck, if I'm honest, it's made me love.

Mila is nineteen, almost twenty, and I can safely say I've fallen in love with her. My feelings for her changed and morphed into so much more over the past three years. We've grown closer than I led my brother to believe. Chatting over text messages and on the phone every now and again, I learned more about this exotic beauty than he knows of her.

Every message, every call hearing about her boyfriends, or shall I call them fuck buddies, drove me insane. Those nights I spent buried in women, but the only one in my mind as I pounded those strangers was her. Mila.

She reaches for me and pulls me closer for our lips to meet once again in a soul-stealing kiss. "I want you," she murmurs. In this moment, my heart wants to beat right out of my chest and into her hands.

Rising, I push off my slacks and boxer briefs. A small gasp falls from her lips at my naked form. My nine inches will make her remember me tomorrow. I climb onto the bed beside her, and her body curls into mine. Her bare skin on mine has me barely holding onto a sliver of restraint. Grinding my teeth, I take a deep breath and hope this isn't going to blow up in our faces. Fear, lust, desire, and frustration fills me as I pull her against me. This woman has captured me more than I could have imagined.

I lie back, tugging her over me. "You ready for me, sweetheart?" I question, and she nods. Her long black hair frames her face. Those deep, forest-colored orbs meet mine, sparkling with need, want, and affection, an emotion that leaves me breathless. Her chest rises and falls, and I can't help feeling the need to lave at her sweet nipples.

She rocks her hips, and the heat of her pussy has me groaning. My hands settle on her hips, allowing her to sink onto me slowly, so fucking slow its torture. The tightness and slick heat of her is incredible. Better than anything I've ever felt. Her body hovers over mine, and her lips mold to my mouth. The kiss is slow, sensual, and before I can do anything, her hips roll against me. She's so inviting. And with one lift of my hips I'm fully seated, as I slip inside the tightest pussy I've ever fucking felt.

My head falls back, and I groan in satisfaction at her body molding to mine.

I want her.

Only her. Fuck.

I'm so fucking fucked.

"Jesus, Mila," I bite out as she rides me. My fucking sweet girl is on my dick, and all I want to do is make love to her. Fucking her once will never be enough. Nothing in my life has ever felt so good.

Even though I'm buried balls-deep inside her, I'm fucking jealous of the men who've been there before me. I want to fuck them from her memory. I don't want any other man with her, and that feeling is so fucking foreign to me, I don't know what to do with it. So, I shut my eyes and revel in the feel of her.

I drive into her, deeper, faster, harder. Reaching out, I find her clit, circling it with my thumb, I feel her pulse and tighten around me. I keep going, plunging into her, claiming her pussy. My body locks when her cunt clamps down on me and sends me spiraling with an orgasm that allows me even deeper inside her.

She cries out and soaks me in her sweetness. Lifting my thumb to my mouth, I lick her honey from it, and I know at that moment; I'm owned. I'm a fucking claimed man, and it's all because of her.

All I want to do is tell her how I feel. To be honest for once in my life, but I don't. I allow us this moment to be. Just be. I allow myself to have her. Because I love her. I'll tell her later. For now, I bask in the afterglow of being with the woman I love.

* * *

"I know." Gabriel stalks into the living room, and I can't turn to look at him. I spent another hour enjoying Mila, and when she passed out, I laid her in the bed and placed a kiss to her forehead.

"You know what?" I question, sitting back on the plush sofa. My body is still tense from what I just did with my niece.

"I'm not stupid, little brother. You're in love with her." His words halt my movement of lifting the tumbler to my lips. "I can see the way you look at her," he confirms nonchalantly.

"There's no doubt I love her." I shrug, hoping to steer him off the conversation, but he doesn't bite.

"You love her more than you should. You look at her like a man possessed, Grayson. I've seen that look. It's how I used to look at her mother. I loved that woman with all that I was, all that I am. When I first saw her, I knew." He sips his whiskey and regards me seriously.

My brother and I haven't always seen eye to eye, but something between us shifts. It stills me, my mind and my heart, because he's looking at me like a man would his equal. Don't get me wrong. Gabriel has always been good to me when I wasn't fucking up, but this is different. It's as if he's finally allowing himself to see that I'm a grown man and not a child.

Nodding, I respond calmly. "I do love her, yes. You're right. Seeing her with other guys was difficult," I confess, gulping my drink.

"Then you should stay the night and see where the day takes you tomorrow. It's Saturday, so take her out, on a date."

His words shock the shit out of me. "What?"

"You heard me," he smirks. "She deserves a man who'll look after her. And you know that if you ever hurt her, you'll have me to answer to. Look, I know we've not had an easy relationship. Things were always strained because I just wanted the best for you, and of course you're stubborn, but you're a grown man, and I can see that she's special to you. There's no denying it, brother." He finishes his drink and watches me intently.

"You're really allowing me to be with her?" Incredulity is thick in my tone because somehow, I don't believe he's letting his little brother — the famous man-whore — get anywhere near Mila. He merely nods, and not giving me more, he pushes off the sofa and heads to the liquor cabinet. He pours another two-finger shot of the smoky whiskey.

"I am," he answers, his back to me. I watch him down the whole shot in one swift gulp. "Don't break her heart, Grayson. I'm warning you. If I see tears on her face, I'll kill you." With that, he turns to face me. "I'm going to bed. Take care of my girl."

I'm left alone with my thoughts of what the fuck just happened.

MILA

The sunshine streaming through the window wakes me with memories of last night running rampant in my mind. My feelings for Grayson slam against my chest painfully when I realize we were taking a step we couldn't come back from.

I saw it in his eyes. He looked at me like *that*. It wasn't the way a man would look at his niece. It was the way a man looks at the woman he could possibly fall for.

When my Uncle Grayson stares at me, his suave

demeanor is full of his sexy smirk. It's enough to unravel me, leaving me panting and needy.

I'm not sure what to do with it. Confusion clouds my mind, but when I feel a hand snaking around me, my body shudders at the tender touch. "It's me, sweetheart," he murmurs.

"Grayson?" We've been on a first name basis for so long it comes naturally to me. What doesn't, though, is opening my eyes and finding him here, in my bedroom.

His short, dark brown hair seems always to look like he's just gotten out of bed. Thick, dark brows frame incredible, deep mocha eyes. Always with a light dusting of stubble on his angular jaw, which makes me quiver with need.

His lips are made for kissing, the top one with a beautiful bow shape, and the lower shaped in a way that makes me crave to bite it.

"Good morning," I murmur, burrowing into his arms. My fingers trail over the bare skin of his chest, which is smattered with just enough hair to make him sexy and masculine, bare to my touch.

"You look so gorgeous when you wake up, sweetheart," he whispers, pressing a kiss to my forehead, like he's done time and again when I was growing up. Only this time, it's different, more intimate. It's strange to see him without a suit on. Since he runs the company with my dad, he's always immaculately dressed in Armani or Gucci. Dress shirts that hug his frame and slacks that beg to be taken off.

Simply put, he's a man-whore. Always has been. The fact that he's in bed with me and not with some random woman from the bar makes me wonder what happened to change him so much.

We didn't get to talk because I completely passed out. Four orgasms will do that to a girl.

"And you . . . Well . . ." My words taper off to silence. What do you say to a man you've just fucked? A man that's not some stranger you met at a nightclub, but your uncle? Well, step-uncle.

"I'm Grayson. There's no need for any more explanation." He chuckles, and the sound rumbles through his chest, turning my core molten. That's what he does, with just one smirk, one glance. Shaking my head, I turn, but he grips me tighter, pulling me against him. "Where do you think you're going?" he murmurs against my neck, sending another wave of heat and desire through me.

"I need to get cof—"

"Here you go, Princess." My stepfather walks in with a knowing smile. Something in his blue eyes twinkle and I wonder how two brothers could be more different. Daddy sets the mug down on the nightstand beside my bed and leans in to plant a kiss on my forehead, which is rather awkward because I'm near enough naked, even if there's a comforter wrapped around me.

Everything feels surreal.

I'm Alice, and I've fallen down the rabbit hole.

Everything is fantasy, and I'm lying here in the cocoon of a man who's feathering soft, sweet kisses on my shoulder. "You taste like honey. I think I need another sample," Grayson growls in his thick accent behind me.

My eyes dart to Gabe, but all he does is offer a smirk.

"Dad." My voice is strained with tension.

"No need for an explanation. I know everything," Dad says as if it's the most natural thing in the world.

I nod, and his gaze darts behind me, and he gestures with his chin.

"I think Grayson needs a coffee refill."

There's something they're not telling me, and I'm too wary of the silent gestures and flitting eyes to feel at ease.

Fear knots in my belly, and I wonder if my dad is about to kill Grayson. Or if he accepts what's happened. Deep down, I hope he does, because I need to tell him, to explain that I love him with all my heart, but that I'm in love with Grayson. I have been for a long time; I just didn't think he would see me that way.

Emotions squeeze my heart painfully, and breathing becomes difficult. I push up and tug the sheet to cover my bare breasts. Grayson silently gets out of the bed and heads to the kitchen, and I can't help stealing a glimpse of his beautifully toned ass in those tight boxer briefs.

"Listen, Princess." Gabe settles on the bed beside me and reaches for my hand. When I slip mine in his, he lifts his gaze to mine. "I spoke to Grayson last night, and . . ." Before he can tell me anything more, the man in question walks back into the bedroom with that confident stride like he's the king of the world. And he could be — everything about him screams power and sex appeal.

"Am I interrupting?" he quips, and with a lift to the side of his mouth, he dons what I've now branded *The Panty Dropper* because god, I would drop mine if

I were wearing any.

"I think you and Mila need to talk." Gabe releases my hand, and my brows furrow in confusion.

"What's going on? Is something wrong?" The alarm in my tone doesn't go unnoticed by either man.

In tandem, they both respond with a confident, "No."

"Okay, then someone needs to tell me what the hell is going on. You're both acting weird." I push off the bed, wrapping the large, gray sheet around my bare body.

"I'll leave you to it." He taps Grayson on the shoulder and calls to me, "See you later, Princess," striding out of my bedroom with a chuckle.

Dragging my gaze to Grayson, I pin him with a glare. "Are you going to tell me, or are you going to stand there with that goddamn smirk on your lips?" I retort, only to earn myself a chuckle. So deep and sexy I can't stop the pulse between my thighs.

"Oh, sweetheart, I'll tell you." He sips his coffee. With his head tipped to the side, he saunters over to me, oozing confidence. One foot in front of the other, he nears me. When we're only inches apart, he leans in so close I think he's about to kiss me, but he doesn't. His mouth whispers along the shell of my ear, "I'm taking you out today. On a date. So put some clothes on, before I fuck you right here against your bedroom window." His drawl drips hunger, the same craving that's swirling just below my belly button.

"You what?" My response is weak, just like my knees, and my head spins with possibilities.

"I'm taking you on a date," he tells me calmly. Stepping away, his gaze holds me hostage.

"I don't understand. I mean, we can't just—"

"We can." He sets his cup on the dresser, and his large hands cup my face, holding me close. "I want you. I've fucking fallen in love with you, Mila." His confession hitches my breath and seeps into my chest, leaving me breathless. Dark brown, almost-black eyes pin me so painfully and beautifully that I can't respond. Words don't come when I open my mouth, and I'm reeling like I've just been winded.

My body is alight with emotion. A maelstrom of everything hits me all at once. Affection, need, and desire. Lust, hunger, and love, that's it — at the forefront is love. Fuck.

"I . . ." My admission disappears in the air around us, hanging above us like a piece of mistletoe. He pulls me toward him, our mouths touching, so lightly it's as if a butterfly's wing is flitting across my lips.

"I love you, Mila. I've always loved you." Honesty rings true in his words, and I recall a memory so poignant in our relationship it stills my heart.

"Hello, Grayson. How is my favorite uncle?" I answer my phone in a hushed tone. It's almost midnight, and I'm sleepy. A year has passed since mom died, and we've slowly grown closer by calls and messages. So, this isn't a surprise that he's calling me. But this late?

"Hi, sweetheart, and I told you, don't call me uncle. It freaks me out," he groans into the phone, and I have to stifle the giggle that threatens to fall from my lips.

"Okay, okay, Grayson. Why are you calling so late?" I roll over. Pushing up, I sit with my back flush against the headboard.

"I missed you," he murmurs into the phone, and the sound has me squeezing my thighs together.

"You're calling at midnight because you missed me?" I question on a giggle, and a groan so low rumbles through the line, and if it weren't so quiet in my room, I would have missed it. My heart thunders in my chest, and I wonder if he would ever feel for me what I do for him. Would he ever want me?

"I did. Just wanted to hear your voice and say goodnight, sweetheart."

The nickname he uses sounds so different when he says it tonight. So . . . Sexual.

GRAYSON

"Grayson, I . . ." Her voice lowers. "I love you too."

The words fall from her lips to mine, and I let out a breath I didn't know I was holding. Crashing my mouth to hers, I kiss her so deeply, so fucking hard, with so much affection, and I want her to know I'm not leaving. I want to tell her all the words I can't say with this kiss.

All my life I've fucked around, I've had a different woman in my bed each night of the week, but right now, the only one I want is standing before me with those green eyes pinned to mine.

"So, will you let me take you out?" I question, hope flourishing when she beams and nods.

"Yes. I can't believe this . . . Isn't it weird?"

Shaking my head, I stare into her eyes for the first time in so long and respond with conviction, "This will never be weird. We've found each other for a reason, sweetheart. You are mine. Do you hear me?" Her gaze darkens, and my heart constricts painfully.

"I'm yours," she agrees, but there's something she's not telling me. It's written all over her face. "I've always been yours." She peers up at me through dark lashes. "Will you join me in the shower?" Her lips lift into a wicked smile, and I know I'll never say no to her.

Without a word, I grip her ass, lifting her against me, and her squeal is enough to have me rock hard. "I'm going to fuck you in the shower, and then we're going out, okay?" She nods, her arms twined around the top of my shoulders and her face nuzzled in my neck.

In the *en-suite*, I set her down on the counter and turn on the shower, then turn to her. She's completely bare to my hungry gaze. Her nipples pebble under my scrutiny, and I can't help but feel proud of this woman that's mine now.

At thirty-two, I'd never have thought I'd be with a woman of nineteen, but there's no one else for me. "Come on, sweetheart, let's get you cleaned up." Shoving my boxer briefs down, I glance at her staring at me. Her gaze rakes over me in the most seductive way, and I'm ready to fuck her senseless.

She hops off the counter and stalks past me into the shower. Her body is utter perfection, flawless with an ass I can't wait to claim.

"You coming?" she taunts, glancing at me over her shoulder.

"I will be. So will you," I promise, stepping under the spray behind her. Grabbing her shower gel, I squirt some into my hand. The scent of candy hits me. It's her, so fucking her. Sweet, and so intoxicating I feel high just from the dollop in my palm. Lathering my hands, I place them on her shoulders, massaging and kneading the muscles.

A whimper falls from her lips and echoes in my ears. Running my hands down her arms, stroking and teasing until I reach her hips, and I see her wince. "What's wrong, sweetheart?" She spins in my arms, and I glance at the word written on her body. "I love that tattoo."

"It was for you," she coaxes in a honeyed tone. Her finger trails a path from my belly button up to my chin, then slowly teases my lips. Swiftly, I snatch her finger between my teeth and bite down on a growl.

"Don't toy with me, sweetheart. I'll spank that little ass." I release her finger and tug her against me. My stiff cock throbs between us. Shocking me, she reaches forward and grips my shaft, stroking slowly, while her eyes are pinned to me.

"And what if I enjoy the spanking?" Her tongue darts out, licking her lips as she purses them in a seductive pout. *Jesus. Fucking. Christ.* This woman is going to be the death of me.

"I'd count on you loving it. Then you'll need a good fucking, and I'll dole that out every fucking day, sweetheart." I lean in and tug her bottom lip between my teeth, biting down, earning myself a sexy moan. "Is my sweetheart wet for me?" I question in a raspy tone.

"I'm drenched, Grayson, just for you." Her breathy words are enough. Without answering, my hands find her ass, lifting her so both legs wrap around my waist. I walk her backward till she's flush with the wall. The tip of my cock nudges her entrance, and I have to ease myself into her tight, slick pussy.

"Jesus." A guttural groan from my lips is all I can manage as I sink into her, fully seated.

Her body pulses and quivers around me, and I'm a man possessed.

"Fuck me, please?" she begs, and I lose all fucking control.

My hips slam into her, faster and harder. So fucking deep, she's clawing at my shoulders. "Mila, sweetheart . . ."

"Oh, Grayson, God, I'm . . . Fuck . . ." Her words tumble out, not making any sense as I plunge into her repeatedly. I need her. I fucking ache for her.

"Mila, come on my dick, sweetheart. Fucking soak me in your sweet honey." My teeth latch onto her smooth, bare shoulder as I growl my order, and she does. She shatters around me, her body quivering, milking my dick for all it's worth, and I can't hold back any longer.

My release hits me full force, and I bite down as she screams out in pleasure, her nails digging into my back, and I don't care if she draws blood. All that matters is that I've just fucking marked her, claimed her, and now I fucking own her.

"Jesus, you're going to kill me, sweetheart," I murmur against her neck, licking at the spot my teeth have marked her. Her body trembles in my arms. Something about it makes me need to see it more, to have her come undone below me again. To have her body writhing in ecstasy as I take her.

"I think you'll survive, Grayson."

Her response is breathy at best, and as I let her down on shaky legs, I wrap her in my arms and tug her under the warm spray. Closing my eyes, I feel the calm overtake me.

Having a moment like this, connected not physically but emotionally is new to me, and my heart thumps wildly. Her hand reaches up, and she places it on my chest, right where she can feel the beat. "Why did you choose me? Why would you put yourself through this?" She lifts her eyes to find mine, curiosity dancing in those green pools.

I know what she means. We're in for a shit storm of note when her mother's side of the family finds out. Mila isn't the easiest girl to live with or to be with. Her father told me about her fiery personality. She's like a live flame, ready to destroy anything in its path.

"I chose you because my heart has been cold for too long. I need your fire, your warmth." I confess my darkest hurt, the pain that I've covered up for too long. A shiver wracks her body, and I realize the water has gone cold.

Turning off the tap, I lift her up and step out of the shower. Setting her down on the woolen rug, I grab two towels and wrap her in one. "Did any of the women you were with ever tell you that you're romantic?" Tipping her head to the side, she regards me with an affectionate gaze.

"No, I'm not. And no, they haven't because, with them, I was a dickhead. I fucked them" — the wince on her face is clear — "but they never managed to find my heart. That was held by someone else a long time ago, and I closed myself off to the idea of ever giving it to someone again." This isn't the place I wanted to confess, to tell her the truth, but here I am.

"And me?" Her mouth pursed into a line. Her confidence falters somewhat. She doesn't realize it, but it's written all over her face. She thinks I'm telling her I don't want her.

"Listen to me, Mila." With my index finger, I lift her chin, so her eyes meet mine. "You're the one who broke through. You and you alone are the girl I want, the one I want to give my heart to. Please, don't ever doubt that." I implore her, begging for her to let me in. She's young, but she's not stupid.

I know all the secrets, all her darkest and most beautiful parts. I know her desires and what she dreams about. Everything about this woman is mine. It's been mine for longer than we both realize, and in turn, I'm hers.

Nothing will change that. Ever.

GABRIEL

As soon as I walk into the office, my mind clears. Last night was too emotional. There was always a possibility in my mind that my brother had fallen for Mila. They didn't realize I knew about the messages and calls. If it wasn't for my brother, I don't think my daughter would have gotten over losing her mother.

Slipping into my chair, I open the lid of my laptop and turn it on. Opening the email program, I pull up the new messages and start flicking through them. Nothing of importance comes through on the weekend, but I wanted to make sure the contracts were finalized.

Sitting back, I wonder where Grayson will take Mila today. Hopefully, he'll stop his womanizing ways and be happy. I saw it last night, the look in his eyes when they sat at the dinner table, and with how he watched her. It was obvious the emotion was more than I could have imagined.

There is love between them. I just hope it's strong enough to withstand everything they'll be challenged with. Not only is there an age gap, but there will be talk in our community of the fact that Grayson is family. Granted, it's not by blood, but I'm guessing Shanika, my deceased wife's sister, and Mila's aunt, will have something to say about it.

Sometimes, when you fall in love, nothing can stop you. I've lived through that when I first walked into their household and told them I was marrying Mila's mother. It took them a long time, but they came to accept it . . . Eventually.

A knock at the door drags my attention from my racing thoughts. Pushing off the chair, I head toward the entrance and push the buzzer. As soon as the door swings open, I'm met with piercing blue eyes, caramel skin, and long dark hair. "Lissy." The gruff tone of my voice startles me.

I've known her since she was sixteen when she flew over from Spain to visit her aunt and cousin in America. Only three years older than Mila, her cousin is an exotic beauty.

"Uncle Gabe," she coos, striding confidently toward me like a tiger on the prowl. *Jesus.* What is it with these girls? "How are you?" She rounds the reception desk and lifts onto her tiptoes to kiss me on the cheek.

"I'm good. What are you doing here?" I take a visible step back, hoping to put some distance between us. After what happened with Mila last night, I need to clear my mind.

"Aren't you glad to see me?" She smiles, her wide grin lighting up her face, and those gems of ice sparkle with mischief as she regards me.

"I am. I'm sure Mila would be too." I turn and head into the offices from the reception area. Her heels click-clack on the marble tiles as she follows me.

"I'm back for good, got into town yesterday. I stopped by the house, but nobody was home, so I figured . . ." She trails off, settling her pert little ass on the edge of my desk. "I'd come here and see you." She laughs again. This time, it's a sultry, sexy smile, and I can't help but notice her outfit isn't one you'd throw on while moving.

"And you decided to dress up as well?" I question, folding my arms in front of my chest as I regard her. The skirt she's wearing rides up her thighs, and my gaze settles on them. My cock hardens gradually as she shifts, and I'm awarded a spectacular glimpse of her pink panties. They're a deep magenta, bright, and I'm dying to rip them off with my teeth.

"I like to look good," she responds on a breathy whisper as my eyes edge their way up to hers — a spark, like the very one between my brother and her cousin, flashes in the air. Like a live wire, it crackles between us, and I know she didn't randomly pop by. She's here for one thing, something I'd love to give her, but I can't. This is ridiculous.

What would people say?

"Gabe," she murmurs. Sliding off the desk, she stops at my knee. She's so close I could tug her onto my lap and lift her skirt over her hips, tear that scrap she calls underwear from her body and drive myself so deep inside her.

I could get lost in her.

"I think you should go, Lissy. I'll let Mila know you're back, and she should call you." When I rise from the chair, I realize it was a wrong move because it puts me inches from her.

The scent of cinnamon and brown sugar hits me immediately. My mouth waters to have a taste, to see if her skin — the color of caramel — really tastes as sweet. "Uncle Gabe." Her murmur stirs something inside me. Deep and unyielding. Something I shouldn't allow myself to feel, but I do. It courses through me, but I can't do this.

"You should head out, sweetheart." I step away from her and take a deep breath. She regards me quietly. Something in my tone must have given away the fact that I don't want her to go, because for a moment, she simply watches me.

It's our silent standoff. And just like her cousin, she offers me a smile that could break a million hearts. I'm too old for her. She's too young for me, but deep down, all I want is to bend her over my desk and drive myself into her tight, young body. "Would you prefer if I called you, Gabriel?" She quirks her brow and her icy-blue eyes shimmer like diamonds. They're like glass orbs, piercing my restraint.

"Jesus, you need to go. Please?" My voice, filled with need and hunger, implores her, but she's stubborn. It runs in the fucking family because Mila is exactly the same.

"Gabriel Connor." Her tone lightens, and she beams. Her face lights up, brighter than any fucking star, and I'm a goner. She's all grown up. No longer the young teenager that used to love popsicles and candy.

Jesus, Gabe.

What are you doing?

"Melissa Reyes, you need to get your pretty little ass out of here." I stalk around her, trying to keep my distance. But her scent is like a fog, like an intoxicating essence made to tempt and lure.

"So, you admit you've looked at my ass?" She giggles behind me, and I shake my head, not taking the bait. I pull open the door and regard her with a small smile.

"I'll see you soon, Lissy." I utter, but using the nickname I gave her when she was younger doesn't help. Looking at her as a woman rather than a girl is easy, because she stands almost at my height with those fuck-me heels she's wearing.

With one manicured nail, she trails it down the front of my shirt, button by button, until she reaches the waistband of my jeans. Thankfully, she stops and leans in, her mouth at my ear. "I'll see you very soon,

Uncle Gabe." And with that, she's gone. Strolling to her little red Mini Cooper.

My gaze is locked on her ass and hips as they sway. My mouth waters for a taste. Just one fucking taste and I know I'll be fucked. So, I turn and head back into the office.

You can't do this, Gabriel.

Grabbing my phone, I hit dial on Brigitte's number. "Darling, are you missing me already? It's only been three days." As much as I need to fuck out my frustration, I wonder if this is a good idea. Everything about this woman screams *marry me*, and that's not what I need.

"I just need to bury myself in someone," I bite out.

"I'm home tonight," she sighs. I knew she wouldn't deny me.

"See you later."

With that, I grab my keys and head out. Staying in this office with Lissy's sweet scent lingering will drive me insane.

MILA

The drive is quiet, and I glance over at Grayson, taking in his profile. The fact that he had a car pick us up so he could focus on me is something I'd have to get used to. Dad normally drives me everywhere, even though he can get a town car to chauffeur us. "So . . ." I don't know why I feel insecure, but Grayson is older. He's used to women, not girls.

He turns to me and wraps his arm around my shoulders, tugging me into the crook of his arm. "So, I love how you fit in my arms. Perfectly. Like you were always meant to be there," he murmurs, planting a kiss on my hair.

"I . . ."

"Look at me." Lifting my gaze to his, those dark pools of desire tighten everything south of my belly button. "You're mine now." He drops his mouth to mine in a soft, sensual kiss. Our lips mold together, fusing with heat and desire. His tongue sweeps into my mouth and duels with mine.

A whimper falls from me, but he swallows it. He inhales me as I do him. As if I'm his breath, his lifeforce, and he needs me to survive. The realization hits me, deep in the depths of my young, teenage heart that this man loves me.

When he finally breaks the kiss, his stare bores into mine. Then he grins. Not the cocky smirk I'm so used to, this one is filled with affection. It's sweet and romantic. "I love how pliable you are in my arms."

"Mr. Connor, we're here," the driver calls from the front of the car. And we're dragged from the cloud we're in.

"Thank you, Graham." Grayson opens the door and exits the car. Turning, he offers me a hand, which I accept. The sun is high, and when Grayson grabs the basket in the trunk, I'm giddy with excitement. "I'll call you when we're ready." And with that, we walk down toward the water's edge. I know I'll be wanting to come out here more often, especially with the man who's made me happier than I've ever been.

We've been in Seattle for almost all my teenage years, and I've never been on a date at the beach. Finding a secluded spot is easy since it's so quiet. "It's so gorgeous out here today." I watch him lay down a blanket. Something too romantic, too intimate. It's a real date.

"Are you going to watch me all day?" he quips, one side of his mouth lifting in that signature smile. The one that sets my heart alight.

"Maybe." I reach for the hem of my tank top. Pulling it off, I launch it at him, and he chuckles a deep, sexy rumble. Shoving my shorts down, they pool at my feet, leaving me in a string bikini. His gaze scorches me as if he's touching me. A slow lick of heat trails from my feet, up my legs, and slowly up to my breasts.

"Jesus, Mila . . ." When those mocha pools meet mine, they're molten.

"I'm going for a swim." I giggle. Toeing off my sandals, I turn and run toward the water. The waves crash against me. It's cooling, but it doesn't calm the fire burning inside me for him. For Grayson Connor.

Diving into the waves, I relish the water. When I break the surface again, I turn to find Grayson standing on the sand inches from where the waves are crashing. "Are you going to come have lunch? Or am I going to come out there and drag you out?" he calls to me with a smile on his face. Warm and inviting.

I pad through the water, pushing my way toward him, and as soon as I have purchase on the sand below my feet, I break into a run. Crashing into his arms, earning me the warmth of his embrace, I nuzzle into his neck, inhaling his cologne, the scent that's him. Only him.

"Cold out there?" He lifts me easily, walking us back to the blanket.

"It's a bit chilly, but it's refreshing. Are you going to join me?" I murmur as he sets me down. Shaking his head, he pulls his T-shirt up over his head, and I take in the taut torso. His chest has a light dusting of hair, dark and masculine. Everything about him screams man.

"I don't swim, sweet cheeks," he tells me with that signature smirk. "Let's eat."

The spread of food is incredible. How he managed this in only an hour, I don't know, but it looks delicious. "You trying to fatten me up?" I quirk, popping my hip and crossing my arms in front of me. His dark eyes trail up my body in a heated gaze.

"Sweetheart, you're going to need your energy for what I have planned, so why don't you eat up?" There's something illicit in his voice, and I can't stop my thighs from squeezing together.

"Am I going to be able to walk tomorrow?" I giggle, but the dark look he pins me with tells me I may not. Those almond-shaped eyes narrow farther, and his bow lips purse in what looks like an air kiss, and I'm dying to feel them on my skin.

"Perhaps, if you're a good girl—"

"And if I'm not?" I ask, kneeling on the blanket, my eyes peering up at him with curiosity.

"I'll have to spank that little ass before I fuck you until you pass out." His words are a vow. A promise I'm willing to see him follow through on.

"Mmm hmm . . ." Lifting an olive from the small bowl, I pop it in my mouth, enjoying the salty flavor. "I bet," I respond in a breathy tone. The surrounding air is thick with desire. How is that since we've opened the floodgates, all I want is to feel him between my thighs?

"You're blushing, Mila," he states matter-of-factly. "Is there something on your mind?"

Shaking my head, I feel the heat of a blush creeping up my neck and onto my cheeks. "Of course not." I don't meet his eyes, the ones that are currently boring a hole into me. Jesus, this man is going to be the death of me.

"Come on." His arm is on me in an instant, tugging me off the blanket.

"What—?"

"I'm going to get you wet," he growls. Leaning in, he throws me over his shoulder, and I can't stop the squeal that falls from my lips. He walks us toward the water, and I'm wiggling in his grip.

"Put me down." I giggle loudly, but my body is tingling all over from his hands on my legs, thighs, and when he rains a spanking on my ass, heat pools in my bikini bottoms.

As soon as we hit the water, he makes his way deep into the ocean, sliding me down his body. The thick erection between his legs prods against me, causing me to moan. "Is this what you wanted? To taunt me?" Shaking my head, I bite down on my lower lip and meet his hooded gaze. "Do you enjoy taunting me, sweetheart? Because I will fuck you anywhere I please."

Wrapping my legs around his taut waist, I press my quivering pussy against his cock, reveling in the feel of him pressing against me. "What are you waiting for?" I tease.

He doesn't answer me. Instead, his mouth crashes on mine, causing my body to shudder with need against him. Our tongues duel, tease, and taunt and when I suck his into my mouth, he groans low and feral.

"Fuck me," I moan against his lips, and he doesn't need more permission. His fingers push my bikini bottoms to the side, finding my hot core.

"Jesus, sweetheart, you're slick and needy," he moans in approval. My hand snakes between us. Shoving the front of his boxers down, I grip his steel shaft and stroke it slowly. "I need to be inside you," he hisses through clenched teeth, and I nod. Positioning him at my heated entrance, he rolls his hips, sliding into me, stretching me deliciously.

"Grayson." His name is a murmur as he drives into me. The waves crashing around us and the pull of his body are like a magnetic force not allowing me to pull away.

"Mila," he moans. My name on his lips is a hoarse whisper full of hunger that matches my own. My nails dig into the smooth skin on his shoulders, marking him. "Jesus, Mila, sweetheart." Words fall into the crashing waves as my body tightens, pulses, pulling him in farther as if we can't get close enough.

"Please, Grayson, I need you . . ." My head drops back on a cry as his mouth suckles on the soft flesh of my neck. My release is so close, coiling, rumbling through me like a hurricane about to unleash an ungodly sound. Grayson bites down on one of my pebbled nipples, and it sends me crashing into the depths.

White stars burst behind my eyelids, and his animalistic growl tells me he's joined me in bliss.

GRAYSON

She's perfect. Everything about her: her smile which lights up her face as she giggles as the water splashes against her legs, and the soft blue bikini hugs her body. Her breasts heave as she runs back toward me. Long, wet hair sticks to her back. Small droplets glistening on her tanned skin have me salivating, wanting to lick them off.

"Are you ever going to get your ass in there?" She giggles, dropping onto the towel beside me. I regard her behind my sunglasses, taking in the vision she is.

"Told you, darling, I don't swim." I lean back on my elbow while she stares me down.

"But you did earlier," she reminds me of our little tryst.

"That wasn't swimming. That was me claiming my woman." My response earns me a soft rosy blush on her cheeks, and I can't help smiling.

"Okay, caveman. What are we doing next?" She pops a cherry into her mouth, and I watch her lips pout as she bites the flesh of the fruit. *Jesus, everything she does turns me on.*

"We're going shopping, and then dinner. Reservations are made. We need to get you a dress and perhaps some shoes if you'd like new ones," I offer. Her mouth falls open in a shocked stare.

"Are you crazy? You can't buy me new clothes for a date."

"I can and I will. Get used to it. Now, dry off before I lick you dry. Let's get going." I push up, tugging on my T-shirt. Watching her towel-dry that delectable skin is enough to have me tenting my goddamn shorts again.

Once we're dried off and dressed, we find the car waiting.

When the vehicle pulls up outside the small boutique, I turn to my girl, who's got the biggest smile on her face.

"You're really buying me a dress?" she questions me incredulously.

Nodding, I open the door and exit the car, holding out my hand for her. "I am. Not only a dress but a complete outfit for the evening." She slips her dainty hand in mine, and I feel like a pauper escorting a princess.

As soon as we step into the store, the sales assistant is beside Mila, whisking her off to try on a multitude of dresses. Settling in the comfortable armchair, I face the changing room so once she's ready I'll get the first glimpse of the selection.

An hour later, we're walking out of the store with two bags, one with her dress and the other with lingerie and shoes. I don't know which one she finally chose, but they all blew me away. Her body is perfection; every curve and slope of her luscious figure was accentuated in the flowing material of every gown she tried on.

"Are you going to show me the dress I'll be taking off later?" I lean in, whispering in her ear, but she rebuffs me, shaking her head and smirking as we head back home. "There are many ways I can taunt the answer out of you," I whisper over her skin, sending a tremble through her, which I can't help loving.

Love.

Who knew I'd be sitting here with my brother's stepdaughter, in love and ready to take on the world? I want to take her places, show her things she's never seen.

* * *

It's almost seven. The car is waiting outside, and I hear it. The soft click of her heels on the mahogany floor. It's a sound that allows my heart to fall into a steady rhythm as she nears me. Her delicate breaths are behind me, and when I turn to see her, my heart stutters. My gaze drags leisurely up, from her shimmery pink toes, to the sparkling silver peep-toe heels, and over the sleek, gray silk of her dress.

It's a simple A line that hugs every curve, accentuated with her flawless, caramel skin teasing me from the slivers in the fabric at her hips. The bust cups her breasts, and the soft, sheer lace that peeps at me from her cleavage teases at something more, just a hair's breadth away.

"Do you like it?" she questions with her glossy lips

lifting into a sultry smile.

A sweetheart.

A seductress.

A woman.

"I more than like it. I fucking love it." I'm the one purring because this woman has me by the balls. She steps down from the last stair, and my arms immediately wrap around her, pulling her flush with my body.

The heat of her sears me. It burns through the material of my jacket, shirt, and onto my skin as if she's touching my bare flesh.

Leaning in, I inhale her scent. Sweet, like candy. I take my fill, trailing my nose from her collarbone, up the curve of her graceful neck, and stopping at the spot just behind her ear. "You're incredibly tempting tonight, Mila. I may have to skip dinner altogether and just stay here, taking you, eating you, fucking you. All night long." My words are gifted with a small shudder that wracks through her body.

The tiny chill bumps that rise on her skin are evidence I'm not the only one affected by our proximity, and I'm dying to do just what I said.

Fuck dinner.

Fuck the public.

Just staying home and fucking her would be a dream come true. But I promised her dinner, and I intend on keeping that promise.

"Come on, caveman, you can't keep me locked up forever." She giggles, swatting my shoulder playfully.

"Oh, but I can, sweetheart." I step away, my eyes holding the promise I could if I wanted to. "But I'll allow you one last foray in public. Let's go." I hold out my hand, which she gratefully accepts, and we head out to the car.

I'm falling.

I've fallen.

I'm a goner.

MILA

Last night with Grayson was something else. I've finally had the date I'd been dreaming about for years, and I'm anxious to see him again.

Grayson: *On my way, sweetheart.*

His message comes through as I think about him, and I wonder if he really can read my mind. I teased him about it a number of times. It's as if he knows how I feel without my telling him.

I don't respond right away, letting my thoughts drift to last night. He was a perfect gentleman, like I always knew he would be. And I wonder where we go from here.

Since Dad is accepting of us, I wonder how everyone else would see the relationship that's blossoming. Even though I wish it were easy, I know it won't be.

"Mila, there's someone here for you," Dad calls to me from the living room. I thought Grayson was on his way, but he wouldn't be here so soon. Pushing off the bed, I make my way into the living room to find Tyron, a boy from school who took me out on a couple of dates, but nothing ever came of it.

"What are you doing here, Tyron?" I glare at him. After walking in on him fucking someone else, I never wanted to see him again, but here he is.

"I want another chance, babe." He steps toward me, and I take one back. "Look, I don't expect you to forgive me right now, but . . ." He stares at me for a moment. "Mila, I love you."

That makes me laugh. I can't help it, but love? "You're serious," I snigger with incredulity dripping from my voice.

"I am. I need you, baby." When he reaches for me, I

can't help but shudder at the thought of his hands on me; hands that were on another woman.

"You need to leave. My dad's in his office with my—"

"And who might this be?" Grayson's soothing tone comes from behind me. Like a whisky, dripping with a smoky growl.

"Uhm, this is Tyron. He was just leaving," I explain, hoping to calm the shit storm that seems to be brewing in the air.

I push away from the wall, and that's when everything fucks up. "Come with me, Mila." Ty's hand grips my wrist painfully. When I cry out, Grayson's body is behind me, close, tugging me back, and that's when I see it. A fist flying in front of me, and I hear the crack. The sound of Tyron's nose breaking echoes through the surrounding space, and as if in a movie, everything plays in slow motion.

Tyron goes down in a split second, and when I spin on my heel, I find Grayson nursing bruising knuckles. "Are you okay?" I reach for his hand, and the hiss of pain startles me. I've never seen Grayson angry, livid in fact. As if he's vibrating with rage.

"Who the fuck is that?" he bites out, pinning me with a glare filled with so much anger I feel it down to my bones.

"He . . . I . . ."

"One of your little fuck buddies?" he bites out, and I flinch at the tone he's using.

"You know what? Fuck you, Grayson! I don't need you to walk in here and act like you suddenly care. I fucked guys, and you fucked women. Do you even know how it felt when I saw you with them?" Prodding a finger in his chest, I'm shocked when he stumbles back. But I don't stop. "Do you? It fucking hurt. It broke me. Every. Fucking. Time. My heart hurt so much the only way I could make it through was to go out and find a 'fuck buddy' as you put it. Because you didn't want me!"

With that, I storm by him toward my bedroom. Once inside, I slam the door and lock it. Leaning with my back flush against it, I slide down, along with the tears that tumble down my cheeks.

"Mila," the deep voice comes from the other side of my door, but I don't answer. I can't. My body wracks with a sob so fucking painful it feels as if my heart is being ripped from my body. "Princess, open the door. It's only me." My dad's tone is soothing, and I manage to push away from the door and unlock it.

When he steps inside, he immediately falls to his

knees and tugs me into his arms. "I . . ." My words can't form. It hurts too much. The agony is unreal. Almost as bad as the day I lost my mother.

"Listen to me." He cups my face in his big, strong hands, making sure I meet his gaze. "That asshole, my brother, he loves you. He only got angry because he was worried about you."

Shaking my head, I push away from him and curl into myself. "He . . . What he said to me was uncalled for." Gabriel sits back on the floor opposite me. He's always been an incredible father, knowing when I needed space and knowing when to push.

He watches me. I can feel his gaze on mine.

"I'm not saying he's right in what he said, but I'm asking for you to give him a chance. Don't let something this small come between something so strong."

His words jolt me from my sadness, and I quickly meet his gaze.

"I'm serious, Princess. I've never seen him this fucked up over a woman. Yes, there've been many, but this is different. I think you need to take a step back and look at it from his perspective as well as yours. No relationship is easy, and for you two, it will be even more difficult, but in saying that, he's as immature as you are, so perhaps you'll both learn from each other."

"Dad, I feel like he's blaming me for Ty coming over when he spent days, nights, weekends here with bimbos, and he doesn't understand how I feel. Like . . . It's the same thing. If he loved me so much, surely he can see that it gutted me as well?"

"He knows. He's not stupid, Mila. Just, give him a chance." I watch those icy-blue orbs corner me, and I can't deny him. Yes, he's my stepfather, he's also one of the most important men in my life. The other being an ass who's probably sitting moping over a double shot of whisky.

"Is he drinking?" I question. My response is the nod I was expecting. "Fine." Pushing off the floor, I help Gabe to stand, and we head out of my bedroom and into the living room, only to find my now-boyfriend flopped on the sofa with a swollen hand nursing his drink.

When he spots me, he flies off the leather cushions, waiting tentatively to gauge my reaction. "Sweetheart." One word, only that one fucking word, and I'm putty in his hands. "I'm sorry. I'm an asshole." Hearing him say it makes me laugh. Almond-shaped eyes, dark brown, pin me to the spot. And then I'm gifted that smirk. The one I would do anything for, and I nod.

"Yes, you're an asshole, a big one," I counter, confirming that he's been acting like a child. Worse than I have. I step forward, waiting for him to make the first move. My body trembles as he reaches for me, but I'm just out of arms reach.

"You two are going to be the death of me. Kiss and make up," Gabe growls behind me, and I can't help snickering. "Mila, Grayson, will you two just relax? You've both got pasts. There are bound to be exes popping up, but it's how you handle them now that counts. Don't let some asshole come between you."

"It's not about the asshole, it's . . ." Grayson's gruff tone is evidence he's in a bad mood about Ty being here, but it's not my fault.

"It's the fact that Grayson doesn't understand that while he's been parading women in here, I've had a life as well. I didn't become a nun and sit at home, Grayson."

His dark eyes blaze with need, with something other than anger. "Sweetheart, please, just understand that I'm a jealous man. I don't like sharing. Especially with pricks like that asshole that was here." His head tips to the side in an endearing way, and I feel the fight slowly seeping from me, leaving me completely and being replaced with an ache.

To be in his arms.

To feel his lips.

To connect in the most primal of ways.

"Fine," I murmur finally, and both men release an audible breath. "I'm tired," I announce, waiting for Grayson to follow, and when he does, he wraps an arm around my waist and presses a kiss on my cheek. "Night, Daddy." I smile.

"Oh, I forgot to tell you. Lissy is back," Dad says with a small smile on his lips. At the mention of my cousin's name, I spin on my heel, leaving Grayson to trail behind me.

"What?"

"Yeah, she came by the office yesterday, and you were so busy I forgot to tell you," he says in a tone laced with desire. I knew my cousin had a thing for him. She made it abundantly clear, and now that she's back, I bet he's going to have a hard time — in more ways than one — reigning in the spark between them.

GRAYSON

One year later

"Come on, Mila. We're going to be late," I call from downstairs. It's her birthday in two days, and I've planned a trip to Paris. She's never been to Europe, and I can't wait to see her face when we land. She finished her finals only two days ago, and with the vacation upon us, whisking her away was something I'd planned months ago.

Moments later, at the sound of her heels clicking

on the wooden steps, I turn to find the woman who seems to take my breath away every time I look at her. "I'm ready," she mumbles, lugging the suitcase down step by step, and I rush to her side to help her.

"Did you pack the whole closet?" I grunt, trying to get the damn thing down.

"No, Grayson. I packed enough so that I don't run out of clothes since I have no idea where you're taking me," she huffs angrily. Mila hates surprises, but I love giving them to her. Every moment of the past year has been something out of those fucking romantic movies.

"Come on, sweetheart." I encircle her against me and tug her into the space under my arm. "You're my sweetheart, and you need to trust me. It's going to be perfect, just me and you and a city to explore."

"Which city?" she asks. Her eyes narrow as she regards me playfully.

Pursing my lips, I plant a soft kiss on her forehead and chuckle. "A city with lights, great food and wine, and some beautiful sights." Another grumpy huff has me laughing as we make our way to the car, waiting to whisk us off to the airport. The private jet should be fueled and ready to leave when we arrive.

Opening the car door, I allow her to scoot in, mainly

because I want to get the incredible view of her ass in those tiny shorts she's decided to wear. Slipping onto the bench seat beside her, I settle back and pull out my phone to check my emails. "No phones on the trip," she commands in a soft tone beside me, and I chuckle in response.

"I'm just making sure your dad has everything before we jet off." I hit send on the message and pocket the thing because I don't need any interruptions. As we pull away from the curb, I place a hand on Mila's thigh and circle my thumb on her smooth skin.

"Are you trying to tease me?" Green eyes meet mine, and I give her a naughty smirk. Shrugging, I continue my ministrations on her thigh, shifting my hand an inch at a time until I'm near her heat.

"Open your legs, baby girl," I murmur in her ear, my breath fanning over her cheek, and my lips whispering on the smooth skin of her face. She doesn't respond with words, but her legs shift so my hand can inch its way farther until my fingers stroke the apex between her thighs.

Her head drops back as I tease her. Soft whimpers fall from her lips, and I lean in, crashing my mouth to hers, swallowing every sound from her. The sweet taste of her is racing through my veins, turning me into a rabid animal, hungry for her.

"Please, Grayson," she begs, pleading with me for release. My fingers strum her pussy through the soft material of her shorts. Our tongues dance and tumble, fighting with need for what we want.

My cock is thick, aching behind my zipper. "This will have to wait," I promise, pulling my hand away. Her glazed stare is filled with the same desire I'm sure is in mine. Not long after I settle back, the car pulls into the hangar, and the sleek, silver jet is parked, ready and waiting.

"Are you going to tell me where we're going?" she asks again, her voice raspy, but I shake my head. Opening the door, I exit the car and help her out.

"You'll see soon enough, my sweetheart." We head toward the aircraft while our driver lugs the suitcases from the car. "Up with you." With a swift spank on her ass, she squeals and runs up the stairs into the belly of the plane.

Inside the jet, we take our seats, her by the window and me beside her. The crew prepares for takeoff, and the hostess brings a small trolley filled with drinks and snacks, offering Mila something. I watch with a smile as she grabs the chocolate muffin, which I knew she would, and a Coke.

Once I've got a water for myself, I lean back and close my eyes, waiting for us to be airborne. "Are you afraid to fly?" Her voice is in my ear, serving to harden my cock further, straining in my jeans. I open my eyes to regard her.

"No, I'm trying to reign in my restraint," I respond gruffly.

"Why?" she teases, sucking chocolate muffin from her fingers, and I have to shut my eyes again, grinding my teeth to keep from gripping her and making her straddle me.

"Because if you keep teasing me with that damn chocolate, you'll be joining the mile-high club very soon, sweetheart," I bite out, meeting her gaze again.

"Well, what's stopping you?" She giggles again, licking her thumb, sucking on it like she loves to suck my cock.

"Jesus, Mila." The jet suddenly hits cruising height, and I can't wait anymore. Undoing the seat belt, I unclick hers and tug her onto my lap. "Hold onto me," I grunt, and she does. Her hands twine around my neck and I pull her up. Stalking toward the back of the plane, I kick open the door to the bedroom and push it shut behind us.

Her giggles echo through the room when we stumble and fall onto the bed. "Grayson," she moans as I tug her tank top off, and once it's on the floor, I make quick work of her shorts. Her smooth skin shimmers in the dim light, and I push her thighs open, inhaling her scent.

She's wet, and when I place a kiss on her material-clad pussy, the taste of her arousal is enough to have my mouth watering. "Jesus, Mila." With one swift tug, I rip off her panties and dive in between her legs, lick and laving at the sweet, slick heat.

Her hips buck and writhe against my mouth. Her fingers tangle in my hair as she tugs on the strands, trying to pull me closer. "Oh, God . . . Grayson . . . Jesus . . ." Her moans are louder, and I'm sure everyone on the plane can hear her, but I don't care. I feast on her like her body is my final meal.

I slide two fingers into her tight heat, crooking them up, I find the spot which pushes her over the edge, and she flies apart below me. She's trembling, and her thighs on either side of my head tighten as she finds her release.

"Mm, fuck, you taste so good, sweetheart." Meeting her darkened gaze, I rise and shove off my jeans and boxer briefs. She scoots up on the bed, propped up on her elbows. She watches me crawl over her with the tip of my cock at her pussy, needing and aching to drive into her.

"Fuck me, please?" She pouts, and I chuckle. Gripping my shaft, I stroke her entrance with the tip, teasing her wet folds, and her hips buck, trying to get me to slip inside. But I continue teasing. "Jesus, Grayson, please?"

I love when she begs.

Slowly, inch by excruciating inch, I slip inside her. Savoring the sensation of our bodies connecting in the most primal way. Rolling my hips, I fill her, feeling her body pulse around me. My mouth molds to hers, and she licks the flavor of her juices from my tongue and lips.

It's erotic, sensual, and so beautiful to feel so connected to someone. We're ready to take the final step marriage. I want it more than anything. Mila is young, she needs to find her footing in her studies, career, and her life. I will never stop her from doing what she wants. But I need to put a ring on her finger.

With that thought in mind, I connect us by thrusting into her. Pulling out, I slam back in. My desire heats my blood, and she rakes her nails down my back. Digging into the skin, earning herself a grunt.

"Faster, please . . ." Her mewls spur me on, and I slide almost all the way out and power back into her, hitting the deepest depths of her body. As if I could get closer to her.

"Mila, I need you to come, baby, please," I bite out. My release is close, and I want her with me. Reaching between us, I circle her clit with my thumb, applying pressure, and just then, her body tightens, pulling me into her, deeper, and my body locks. "Come for me, sweetheart, come all over my cock." My words send a surge through her, and she smirks. Her body shudders as a release rushes through her, dragging me along with her, and I fill her with my seed.

Her eyes flutter closed, her cheeks are flushed, and her body trembles below me. Leaning in, I plant soft kisses from her breasts up to her neck, suckling on the flesh, causing her to shiver. Soft moans, whimpers, and unintelligible words fall from her lips.

When I reach her ear, I breathe the words, "I'm yours forever, sweetheart. Always and forever." I lift my head, meeting her stare, which is filled with love and adoration.

"And I am yours, Grayson Connor." The words I've wanted to hear for far too long wind themselves around my heart causing it to thud wildly in my chest.

"Good girl. I think it's time I got you a little gift. Something to show everyone you're mine." Her eyes widen at my words. We're still connected as I soften and slip from her. "Today, I'm buying you a ring," I tell her.

She has no choice, because she is mine.

Her mouth opens, and she utters three words I'll never forget.

"I can't wait."

EPILOGUE

The knock on the door makes my heart leap into my throat. I haven't seen my Aunt since Grayson and I got together. Her job has her traveling all over the world, but now that she's back in Seattle, she's wanted to meet up for weeks. Each time she's offered to come by, or invited me for lunch, but I've told her I was busy.

There's no more hiding.

Pulling open the door, I find my aunt, who looks exactly like my mom standing on the threshold of the house where I grew up. When I told her to come here, I was hoping being in the familiar surroundings would ease the news I'm about to deliver.

"Mila," she pulls me into a hug, holding me so tight, I can't breathe.

"Aunt Shanika," I smile. Shutting the door behind her, I lead her into the living space.

Her long dark hair is pinned back, so her face isn't hidden by the curtain of black locks that usually frame her expression. She's nothing like my mother - serious, almost cold and distant. But this hug is something else.

"I've spoken to Gabriel," she tells me as she settles on the sofa, and I take a seat on the opposite couch. I know she's heard about Grayson and me. There's no other reason she would be here.

"Okay," I say, dragging out the word, unsure of what to tell her.

"At first, I was shocked, to be honest, I thought it was disgusting that you're in love with Grayson," she utters, her voice is low, but there's no menace to it, and I wonder where she's going with this.

I bite back a retort. I want to defend myself, defend the man I love. The ring that's on my left hand is painfully clear where my life has taken me. And even though I'm starting a career soon, and Grayson is supporting me following my dreams, I also would like her blessing.

"Your mother was very much a free spirit," my aunt says with a fond smile. "That's where we differed. She was always off doing something exciting, upsetting our folks. But there's one thing I can say, is that I've always admired her."

"She never told me any of this," I whisper, feeling the tears prick my eyes at her reminiscing.

Aunt Shanika nods, "You're so much like her. And I know, deep down, she would've been happy, as long as you were. If Grayson is the man who looks after you, makes you smile every day, and gives you the support you need, then I guess it's okay."

I'm on my knees, holding her close. My heart is filled with warmth and happiness. It's all I ever wanted.

"Is he good to you?"

I glance up at my aunt and nod. "He is. He's the best man, I promise I'll always look after myself, but I can't stop loving Grayson."

"Then we'll have to plan the wedding." Her smile is everything to me. It brings me the comfort in knowing I have my family near, and I have the man I love to spend the rest of my life with.

* * *

Thank you for reading Tempting Grayson! I hope you enjoyed the steamy, taboo story. Not sure what to get next? Why not try Deviant? A student teacher romance with a hint of suspense and a dash of taboo.

ALSO BY DANI

Visit Dani's website for
a full list of her incredible titles

www.danirene.com/books

ABOUT DANI

Dani is a *USA Today* Bestselling Author of seductive and deviant romance.

Her books range from the dark to emotional, but every hero is alpha, and each heroine is strong-willed, bringing the men down to their knees.

She now lives in the UK, after moving from Cape Town, with her better half who does all the cooking while she writes all the words.

When she's not writing, she can be found binge-watching the latest TV series, or working on graphic design. She has a healthy addiction to reading, tattoos, coffee, and ice cream.

www.danirene.com | info@danirene.com

FIND DANI ONLINE

Join my reader group!
www.facebook.com/groups/danisdeviants/

Sign up for my newsletter https://bit.ly/DaniVIPs

BookBub: http://bit.ly/DaniBookBub
Facebook: http://bit.ly/DaniFBPage
Instagram: http://bit.ly/DaniIG
Goodreads: http://bit.ly/DaniGoodreads
Amazon: http://bit.ly/DaniAmazon
TikTok: http://bit.ly/Dani-TT

Made in United States
Orlando, FL
11 August 2022

20867587R00081